Christmas Lemonade

Written by Ralphine Childs
Edited by Ariana Torres-Medley & Carol Hanisch
Illustrated by Samantha Harris

JaRa Publishing
Copyright 2015

Kendra,
thanks for your love &
support over the years!
Merry Christmas!

Ron

For information regarding permission write to:

JaRa Publishing
342 Loughran Court
Kingston, NY 12401
ralphine@gmail.com

Library of Congress Cataloging-in-Publication Data
Christmas Lemonade by Ralphine Childs

ISBN 9780972411417
51000 >

9 780972 411417

This book is dedicated to my hometown, Kingston, a city in the Hudson Valley region of New York, where there are many opportunities for artistic expression and cultivation.

The area is teaming with established and up and coming artists, with inspiring performances from music to drama to visual arts. Some have even chosen this area as their home. The sights and sounds of local artisans can be experienced weekly. The Ulster Performing Arts Center (UPAC) and the Bardavon are theatres that host many artists and some of the most amazing events. If you're ever in the area check out a show at any of these venues. You'll be glad you did!

The area is perfectly nestled right smack dab in the middle of the action of Horse Shows in the Sun (HITS). People from all over the country come to experience these thrilling equestrian events.

With its own nod to history, the Hudson Valley tastefully celebrates its heritage. Reenactments of noteworthy events and museums, such as the Vanderbilt Mansion National Historic Site, are meticulously designed to honor the events of meaningful times gone by.

There are a number of breathtaking murals and sculptures dotted around the region. Many of these pieces are by local artists and leave tourists with an unforgettable visual impression of the magnitude of the talent that is in the area.

The Culinary Institute of American in Hyde Park, a world renowned culinary arts school, offers its students a first class education and is so stellar that aspiring chefs from all over the world are enrolled and diners may enjoy its several restaurants that are open to the public.

Actually, this whole area is chock full of amazing restaurants so tantalizing that people travel rom other states to indulge. Specialty eateries range from award winning restaurants like Deising's Bakery and Sunrise Deli, which offer authentic European and Brooklyn-style pastries, to intimate cafes like Ecce Terra which serve unbelievably tasty Mediterranean cuisine in a cozy setting.

Unique businesses also add to the destination appeal of this neck of the woods. "Bop to Tottom," for example, offers an unusual clothing and accessory line with such detailed artistry and imagination that patrons are sure to walk away with a one-of-a-kind purchase.

No place is perfect but this area gets it right on so many levels. The Hudson Valley is located close enough for a day trip to any of the more metropolitan areas. Entrepreneurs and industries find it prime location to start or grow their businesses as they, too, have access to the amenities of the tri-states (New York, New Jersey, and Connecticut), while enjoying the comforts of an environment with a safe, friendly, small-town-feel.

People here experience the majesty of all four seasons: the winter paints a canvas of grays and whites that provide the perfect backdrop for the powdery snow and ideal skiing opportunities. Then, as winter morphs into spring, the beautiful flowers and trees come to life as they perfume the air and brim like a fresh pot of coffee. There is a sense of awakening during this season that adds to the fresh air atmosphere.

As summer arrives, kid-friendly attractions are at the ready with summer fun activities for the entire family.

In time, as the leaves begin to change colors and the air gets a little chill, fall arrives. The Headless Horseman's Hayrides and Haunted Houses, one of the area's premier fall attractions, provides its guests with a show stopping, heart pounding fright fest. People literally line up for miles and have to be shuttled in to take part in these wildly popular adventures.

Fall also offers the freshest and most colorful seasonal produce that comes from endless acres of apple orchards, pumpkin farms, and farmer's markets. Stunning natural beauty paints the region and is a must see. The Walkway Over The Hudson is one of the best attractions to capture the brilliance of nature's autumn colors. No place has more spectacular foliage than this area in the fall, the season when this story begins to unfold in my hometown of Kingston…

*A special thanks to
all the children and adults who
were involved in the actual
"Christmas Lemonade" experience
upon which this story is based.
Also,
thanks to the Bruderhof
for your amazing support.*

Once upon a time
Not too long ago,
Came a tale by design
From a place you should know.

In upstate New York
Where mountains surround,
Is a place called Kingston,
A quaint little town.

The city was filled
With fun things to do.
There was an arts program
For kids after school,

Where staff were inspiring
And emphasis gave,
A drama arts training
To kids every age.

Now James and Marie
Were the leaders in charge.
Their creative skills
Just set them apart.

They served with a passion
This program indeed,
And at its foundation
Kindness was key.

James and Marie
Worked with the kids,
To prep them for show time
There's so much they did.

They challenged their staff
To make learning fun,
And their dedication
Was second to none.

Each year they planned
A really big show.
The fall was their best
Season, you know.

They'd chosen a play
An old classic story,
With wonder and whimsical
Splendor and glory.

September approached
The start date was near,
The prep time for Christmas
Was finally here!

They'd made all the plans
For the holiday show.
They spread the word quickly

"Get ready, set,
GO!"

They flooded the town
With posters and flyers,
And advertised swiftly
Right down to the wire.

The flurry was fierce
For this great endeavor.
They felt this would be
Their best Christmas ever!

As parents discovered
This well known rendition,
They wanted their kids
To go and audition.

The day for the sign-ups
Had finally come,
And when the doors opened
They knew they'd have fun!

Young children came
From everywhere,
Kids from the neighboring
Small towns were there.

The crowd was amazing
On opening day,
So many had come
To join the new play.

14

They all had shown up
For one simple thing--

**To celebrate Christmas,
To dance and to sing!**

Now each child was certain
To get a key role,
No matter how shy
No matter how bold.

The teachers worked hard
At molding their gifts,
The kids had a blast
While reading their scripts.

But in this town lived
A strange man named Ned.
He had a huge need
To keep his pride fed.

He was very awkward
Around folks he met,
And when disappointed
Was always a threat.

Ned had worked well
With this arts group before,
But one day had a clash
And stormed out the door.

Ned was embarrassed
And felt so dejected,
With no resolution
His mode was infected.

He tried several things
To make them look bad,
He went to great lengths
And not just a tad.

They never struck back
Though insults were thrown,
They simply wanted
To be left alone.

Ned sneaked to discover
Their plans for the show,
And wondered, "Without me,
How well could things go?"
He constantly thought,
"What will they do?"
He stayed to himself
With much time to stew.

Unknown to Ned
The program was flowing,
Excitement was high
Involvement was **growing!**

Attendance had peaked
At one hundred and three,
Plus parents and staff
With James and Marie.

Ned soon got wind of
The program's success,
Becoming more jealous
His conscience a mess.

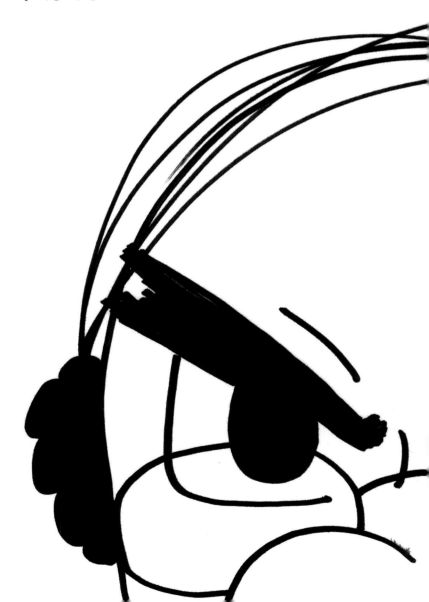

To stop the kids' show
He must find a way,
To steal and destroy
Their holiday play!

He thought of a plan
His most shameless yet,
    He figured a way   As he surfed the net.
                          Contact the writers...
                          And have the show stoppe

    Put them in a pinch
    An extra tight spot.
    He'd bring them to ruin
    There'd be no kids' show,

Destroy their whole Christmas
And no one would know!

"I've got them now!"
Ned said on that day.
He'd just found a way
To crush their kids' play.
"I'm sure they are finished,"
He thought to himself,
"They're all out of business
With no one to help!"

Meanwhile the staff
Nor kids had a clue,
What Ned in his mischief
Was fixing to do.

Early one morning
A beautiful day,
The blue birds were chirping
No clouds on the way.

33

James and Marie
Were up out of bed,
Having some coffee
And freshly baked bread.

They spoke of the play,
It was going so well...

Then suddenly rang
A **startling** bell.

The mailman delivered
A card certified,
The classic play's writers
Had been notified:

"CEASE AND DESIST!
This charge must be heeded."
To do the kids' play
Permission was needed.

"Stop the production
And all the promotion,
Whatever you're doing
Cease every notion!"

So dire and hurtful
Was this sudden news.
"There's only two weeks
'Til show time ensues!"

This problem was pungent
Like lemons we eat.
The bad news was sour,
Somehow bittersweet.

They didn't know
That clearance was needed.
Was this Ned's doing?
Were they defeated?

James and Marie
Stood in their kitchen,
Grappling with thoughts
Their dreadful position.

Needing a miracle
Some good to come through,
Then something happened,
Came out of the blue.

A crazy idea
Came with great speed.
It helped them to see
How to proceed.

They instantly thought
Of a really cool plan,
But knew that they needed
A huge helping hand...

Perhaps they should tell
What happened that day,
Make merry their hardship
Create a NEW play.

Plans were then made
With time of the essence.
They'd learned on that day
A most crucial lesson.

The next day was practice
They met with the parents,
And shared what had happened
The awful occurrence.

A meeting was held
To count up the cost,
Of all the promotion
And show that was lost.
Suggestions for drives
Bake sales at the mall,

Ideas just kept coming
The best one of all:
Tell what happened
And share their great lesson,
The show was the platform
Was this fluke a blessing?

This plan was ingenious
Which all had OK'd,
Though lemons were given
They made lemonade!

As their story spread
Throughout their small town,
Creative ways
To help them were found.

They turned things around
With help from so many,
Support was outstanding
Donations were plenty.

The children sold tickets
The show was now new.
The ticket-sales-meter

Just grew,
and just
grew!

53

Rehearsals were thrilling
And joy filled the air,
The climate was festive
With hope everywhere!

Soon the night came
or the new Christmas show,
The kids were excited
The setting aglow.

They took time to tell
Their holiday plight,
Enacted the plot
On stage that night.

With artistic ways
To dance and to sing,

They shared their true story
It was amazing!

Their thirst for success
Was now satisfied,
The sweet taste of triumph
Refreshed and revived.

Ned hadn't stopped it
This show was the best.
He'd thrown them some lemons,
A character test.

By not giving up
Not letting things cave,
They took their misfortune
And made lemonade!

You can't ruin Christmas
By closing a show,
That's not how it works
And now you must know.

Sharing and caring
The best gifts of all,
Not holiday presents
Or things from the mall.

What happened that year
Will never get old,
This holiday story
Must always be told...

The children that year
Learned a meaningful lesson,
One that is filled with
Abundance of blessings.

At Christmas time
Share this message of hope,
Teach kids resilience
And help them to cope.

Instead of just quitting
When messes are made,
When life throws you lemons
Just make lemonade!